Baby Bear
and the
Long Sleep

Baby Bear
and the
Long Sleep

ANDREW WARD

Illustrated by John Walsh

An Atlantic Monthly Press Book
Little, Brown and Company
Boston   Toronto

Second Printing

Library of Congress Cataloging in Publication Data

Ward, Andrew, 1946-
   Baby Bear and the long sleep.

   "An Atlantic Monthly Press book."
   SUMMARY: Baby Bear has difficulty settling down
for the long winter sleep.
   [1. Sleep—Fiction. 2. Hibernation—Fiction.
3. Bears—Fiction] I. Walsh, John, 1945-
II. Title.
PZ7.W186Bab   [E]   79-21392
ISBN 0-316-92197-1

ATLANTIC-LITTLE, BROWN BOOKS
ARE PUBLISHED BY
LITTLE, BROWN AND COMPANY
IN ASSOCIATION WITH
THE ATLANTIC MONTHLY PRESS

HOR

*Published simultaneously in Canada
by Little, Brown & Company (Canada) Limited*

PRINTED IN THE UNITED STATES OF AMERICA

To
Jake and Casey

THE FIRST SNOW came sifting out of the sky on an early December night, after the trees had dropped their last leaves and all the smart birds had flown south.

"Well, Mother," declared Father Bear, watching the weather from his window, "I do believe it is time for bed."

"So it is, Father," replied Mother Bear, stretching and yawning at her loom.

But Baby Bear, who was building a Bat Bear space station parking garage and rocket launcher speedway headquarters, didn't feel at all sleepy. "Can't I play just for five more minutes?" he asked his parents.

"*Two* more minutes," said Father Bear, setting the table for next spring's breakfast as Mother Bear went from room to room, closing all the window shutters.

After his bath, Baby Bear got into his cowboy pajamas and began to bounce on his bed. He always felt excited after a bath and had a hard time settling down.

"Settle down," Father Bear told him, sitting on his son's bed and picking up a book. "Now then, since you're going to go to sleep for four months, I'll read more books than usual," he announced.

"And some comics, too?" asked Baby Bear.

"I don't read comics," said Father Bear. "Now how many books shall I read to you?"

"A hundred thousand and forty-seven," said Baby Bear.

"Don't be silly," said Father Bear. He thought for a moment. "I'll read eighty-two," he decided, "and not one book more."

THE FIRST BITE'S BEST

It took Father Bear several weeks and days to read all eighty-two books, because bears are slow readers, especially in the winter. By late December Father Bear was getting hoarse, and some of the books, especially the rhyming ones, were making him sleepy.

But none of them made Baby Bear sleepy. He listened to each one carefully, and asked questions about all the pictures, and whenever Father Bear tried to skip some pages to hurry things up, Baby Bear made him go back and read each page all the way through.

"*The End*," Father Bear declared, slamming the last book shut.

"Won't you read just one more story?" asked Baby Bear. "Please? I'll be your best friend."

"You're always my best friend," said Father Bear, kissing his son goodnight.

When Mother Bear came in to tuck in his crazy quilt, Baby Bear asked, "Will you sing me some songs? I'll go right to sleep if you sing me some songs."

"I'll sing thirty-five songs," said Mother Bear, sitting on the edge of his bed. "But only if you close your eyes and try to sleep."

Mother Bear had a beautiful singing voice, especially for a bear. She sang songs about horses and butterflies and meadows, about tired lumberjacks and elephants and sweet potatoes, but every time she paused to see if Baby Bear had fallen asleep he would snap open his eyes and lift up his head and tell her to keep singing.

Mother Bear finished her last song in early January and then bent down and kissed Baby Bear goodnight.

"Leave the light on," Baby Bear said as Mother Bear headed out of his room.

"I'll leave the hall light on," Mother Bear told him.

"But I'm afraid of the dark."

"That's silly," Mother Bear told him. "Just close your eyes and go to sleep and try not to be afraid."

Baby Bear tried not to be afraid, but you know how hard that is. Once you start thinking you're afraid, it's very hard to stop. It's like trying to stop thinking about a rhinoceros in an elevator. For just as long as you try not to think about a rhinoceros in an elevator, there he'll be, clear as day, blinking as the floor numbers light up over the door.

For a whole week, while the moon and sun took turns outside his window and the winter wind rattled his shutters, Baby Bear tried to keep his eyes closed so he

wouldn't see any scary things in the shadows of his room. But keeping his eyes closed just made everything seem darker and scarier than ever.

He imagined blind skunks skulking beneath his bed; giant, hairy bees with silver stingers bumping through the pantry; terrible, golden-locked and lipsticked little girls creeping past the door.

"Papa!" Baby Bear called out, sitting up in bed.

From his parents' room he could hear his father saying, "I got him last time," and then his mother saying, "It's your turn, remember? I sang him all those songs last month."

There was some creaking and some thumping and after a while Father Bear, his ears bent and his eyes puffed, grumped into Baby Bear's room.

"What is it?" Father Bear asked.

Baby Bear wanted to tell his father that he was afraid of the dark, but now he was even more afraid of his father, who didn't like being awakened, especially in January. So Baby Bear said, "Can I have a glass of water?"

"If I give you a glass of water, you'll wet your bed," said Father Bear.

"No, I won't," Baby Bear insisted, feeling a little insulted.

Baby Bear felt better listening to his father's slippers flap along the floor as Father Bear went to fetch the water, and he enjoyed the noise the faucet made as it gushed water into his toothbrush mug, and he liked having his father back in the room, scaring away the skunks and bees and sneaky little girls. The only trouble was that he didn't like water very much and took only a little sip.

"You mean to tell me you got me out of bed just for a little sip of water?" Father Bear roared down at him.

"But if I drink any more," Baby Bear said, thinking fast, "I'll wet my bed."

"Ooo!" Father Bear exclaimed, and he raged out of the room.

"There," Baby Bear said with a sigh, lying back and crossing his legs. "Now I feel a whole lot better." He did not, however, feel any sleepier. "Better," he repeated, enjoying the sound of his voice. "Bet-ter. Better. Better Butter. Better butter bitter batter."

"Hey," he said quietly, sitting up in bed. "Better butter bitter batter. I feel better eating butter. But if it's bitter," he said, raising one claw, "I'll eat batter, even though the butter's better. As I said in my last letter, even bitter butter's better. But her butter's better bitter so I bit her baby-sitter."

Baby Bear wasn't making very much sense, but he was beginning to make a lot of noise: so much noise that he didn't hear his mother flomp out of bed and stamp into his room.

"So," Baby Bear continued, standing up on his bed and waving his arms around. "I bought her water from her otter, who forgot her teeter totter. But her daughter caught her blotter—"

"QUIET!" Mother Bear bellowed, so suddenly that Baby Bear lost his balance and tumbled out of bed.

"Do you realize that the winter's almost over and you're still awake?" Mother Bear said, standing with her paws on her hips.

"I'm sorry," Baby Bear said, scrambling back into bed.

"If I hear another peep out of you this winter, I'm going to trade you in on a new model," Mother Bear said, roughly tucking him in. "Now lie down and go to sleep."

Baby Bear lay still for almost a month, for if there were anything in the world he didn't want, it was to be traded in. The more he thought about it, the more terrible it sounded. He imagined a place where bears traded babies and saw himself standing alone in a dark and snowy lot with a sticker on his nose as his parents walked away with a new baby bear who was guaranteed to sleep.

By late March, Baby Bear was crying, and almost as soon as he started to cry, Mother Bear and Father Bear, looking very tired, were back in his room.

"You know why you're crying?" Mother Bear asked, sitting on the edge of Baby Bear's bed.

Baby Bear was crying too hard to answer.

"Because you're tired," Mother Bear said, reaching out and patting him on the shoulder.

But this just made Baby Bear cry harder, because Baby Bear, like everyone else, hated to be told he was tired, especially when he was.

"Now calm down," Father Bear said, "and tell us what's wrong."

It took Baby Bear a whole day to calm down enough to tell his parents that he was crying because he never wanted to leave his mother and his father and his house and his Bat Bear space station parking garage and rocket launcher speedway headquarters.

"We'd *never* trade you in," Mother Bear said. "That's just something grownups say when they're angry and sleepy. We love you more than anyone in the world. Now stop crying."

"Besides," Father Bear said with a twitch of his nose, "I think I can smell grass sprouting."

Baby Bear sat up and wiped his eyes as Mother Bear went to the window and opened the shutters, and sunshine spilled into the room.

"Right you are, Father," said Mother Bear after a deep breath of morning air. "And will you look at the buds on those trees!"

"Well then, family," declared Father Bear with a quick smack of his lips, "it's high time we all got up and had French toast."

"With honey on it?" asked Baby Bear.

"With honey on it," replied Mother Bear.

So Baby Bear got out of bed and Mother Bear and Father Bear went to their room to dress for breakfast. Then Mother Bear squeezed oranges for juice and Father Bear beat the eggs for the French toast. When everything was ready, Father Bear and Mother Bear sat down at the table. "Baby Bear?" Father Bear called out. "It's time for breakfast."

Baby Bear was having a little trouble getting into his favorite T-shirt because he'd grown so much over the winter and now his clothes were a little small for him. "O.K.," he called back. "I'll be down in a minute."

It took him a little longer than a minute, though, to get into his railroad boots and his holster and his overalls and his Bat Bear cape.

"Mom?" he asked as he made his way downstairs. "Can you snap my pants?"

But his mother didn't answer.

"Mom?" Baby Bear repeated, stopping in the kitchen doorway.

But his mother only groaned a little. She and Father
Bear were both sound asleep, their heads resting on their
soft, warm stacks of toast.

"Never mind, Mom and Dad," Baby Bear whispered. "I can snap them myself." So he did that, and then quietly ate his breakfast as the spring sun rose outside the window.